the MiSADVeNTUReS of

the ANGRY ALLiGATOR

Tony Penn

Illustrated by Brian Martin

BOYS TOWN.
Press

Boys Town, Nebraska

Published by the Boys Town Press
14100 Crawford St.
Boys Town, NE 68010

BOYS TOWN
Press

For a Boys Town Press catalog, call **1-800-282-6657**
or visit our website: **BoysTownPress.org**

Publisher's Cataloging-in-Publication Data

Penn, Tony, 1973-

The misadventures of Michael McMichaels : the angry alligator / written by Tony Penn ; illustrated by Brian Martin. Boys Town, NE : Boys Town Press, [2015]

pages ; cm.
ISBN: 978-1-934490-94-5

Audience: grades K-6.
Summary: Michael McMichaels is a precocious and adventurous third-grader, whose active imagination and flare for the dramatic turns his adventures into MISadventures. In this story, Michael misbehaves on a school field trip. The web of lies he spins to get out of trouble only pulls him further in, and entangles his friends and parents as well. This comical yet educational tale shows the importance of owning up to your mistakes, being honest, and making apologies.--Publisher.

1. Truthfulness and falsehood--Juvenile fiction. 2. Honesty--Juvenile fiction. 3. Apologizing--Juvenile fiction. 4. Interpersonal communication in children--Juvenile fiction. 5. Interpersonal relations in children-- Juvenile fiction. 6. Children--Life skills guides. 7. [Honesty--Fiction. 8. Apologizing--Fiction. 9. Behavior--Fiction. 10. Interpersonal communication--Fiction. 11. Interpersonal relations--Fiction. 12. Conduct of life.] I. Martin, Brian (Brian Michael), 1978- II. Angry alligator.

PZ7.1.P456 M472   2016
[Fic]   1601

BOYS TOWN
Saving Children   Healing Families

Boys Town Press is the publishing division of Boys Town, a national organization serving children and families.

10 9 8 7 6 5 4 3 2 1

For my mom, Karen

Chapter 1

I'm Michael McMichaels, third-grader. The only thing you need to know about me is that sometimes MY LIFE STINKS! It can stink even worse than my Dad's feet. When we watch TV, Dad will stick his smelly feet in my face and laugh. Then Mom rolls her eyes and sighs, "Sweetie, stop that already?"

Parents can be so weird!

Anyway, back to me and my sometimes stinky life. You see, the thing is, I really thought I was going to get eaten by an alligator in my sleep. That's when I decided I wasn't going to sleep again—ever!

It all started during a school trip to the zoo. I was standing with my classmates in front of the alligator pond. Our teacher, Miss Mitchell, was blabbing to a couple of really serious kids. While they were going on and on about where alligators live, what they eat, and all that, I had an idea—an idea I had to share with my best friend!

"Hey, Kenny," I whispered. "How much money will you give me if I throw this rock at that ugly alligator?"

"I don't have any money, Mikey, and I don't think you should. What if you hurt the alligator or it gets mad? Besides, you'll be in so much trouble if someone sees you," he whispered back.

Kenny's one of those nervous Nellies who never wants to do anything fun. So, I shrugged him off.

I had a nice little rock in my hand, waiting for just the right moment to strike. That ugly old alligator won't mind if I toss this tiny rock at him, I thought. Still, I felt a bit nervous.

Miss Mitchell was still blabbing to those serious kids. It's incredible how they're always asking questions and making serious faces.

Anyway, when no one (except Kenny) was looking, I hurled the rock at the gator. I thought my aim was off, and I'd miss by a mile. Guess what? The rock smacked right into that big snout of his!

Boy, did that make the ugly gator mad! He charged at me, running and growling all the way up to the fence. Who knew alligators were so fast! Or loud!

He made such a ruckus, the whole class and Miss Mitchell turned and looked at him. Everybody got a little scared.

It was a good thing that fence was there, or the gator could have chomped us to bits! I bet he could have eaten us all in one bite like we were mozzarella sticks or tater tots.

"Who did that? Who threw that stone?!" shouted Miss Mitchell.

I couldn't believe she saw the rock, but I was glad she didn't see who tossed it. My heart pounded in my chest. I was so nervous!

"Michael, was it you?" she asked me, demanding an answer. Her hands were on her hips, and her face was all scrunched up. "It looked like it came from your direction."

Ugh! What was I to do? I was shaking and had to come up with an answer.

"Um, no, um, it wasn't me," I sputtered. "It was one of the fifth-graders over there."

"Really?" she asked. "Which one?"

I looked at Mr. Miller's fifth-grade class and pointed at the first boy I saw.

"It was him," I told Miss Mitchell and pointed at the boy whose hair was as red as a fire hydrant. Right away, I felt bad.

"Thank you, Michael, for being so honest. I'll tell Mr. Miller right away. What a terrible thing to do, throwing a rock at a poor, defenseless animal. I hope that young man doesn't make things worse by lying about it."

Uh-oh! That's what I just did! I threw a rock at a defenseless creature, and I made it worse by lying. How would I get out of this mess? Please let there be a remote control or an app that can erase what I did!

Chapter 2

On the bus ride back from the zoo, Kenny and I sat up front by the teachers and parent chaperones. Man, it was a good thing there were adults on the bus. Seriously, I think they saved my life!

You see, Mr. Miller's fifth-grade class was on the bus, too. Those kids looked like giants. I kept my eye on the "big redhead," the one I blamed for throwing the rock. I was scared he would try to get back at me for blaming him.

The whole ride, the redhead glared at me. He had a mean, gator-like grin on his face.

I made it back to school with no problems and was trudging into the building when I was tapped on the shoulder. I turned around, and there he was.

The big redhead with the alligator grin stood chest to chest with me.

"So, you told my teacher I threw a rock at that gator, huh?" he growled. He looked really mad—madder than the alligator.

"Um, um, yeah, I guess so. It's not my fault though. I didn't know what to do," I stammered. "I just panicked after I threw it. It was supposed to be a joke, really. Ha-ha!"

"It's not funny, you little jerk. Mr. Miller said he's going to call my parents and tell them I did it. You're dead, you stupid brat. I mean it!"

I was so scared, I really thought I was going to pee my pants. And I hadn't done that since kindergarten. (Well, there was that one time in first grade, too. But it was just a little, so that doesn't count.)

I stood frozen and silent like a flagpole in winter. Finally, I said, "I'm sorry. I didn't mean to get you in trouble."

"It's too late for sorry. You lied, and you're going to pay," he barked.

"Really, how much?" I asked, as I reached into

my pocket. "I have two quarters on me."

"I'm gonna beat your butt," he huffed, "for free."

I laughed nervously and said, "Oh, I can't afford that even at such a good price. How about I give you ten dollars and a video game? I have a bunch to pick from. They're awesome!"

"Listen loser, I'm not joking. Either I'm going to get you at school, or that alligator will get you in your sleep for what you did," he shouted.

"What do you mean the alligator will get me in my sleep?" I asked, as my legs wobbled with fear.

"He's gonna get you for hitting him with that rock. Don't you know alligators stalk their prey at night when

their victims are sleeping? Didn't you read the little sign with all the gator facts on it? It said that's
how they catch their prey. I guess you were too
busy throwing rocks and blaming me!" Then he

scowled and walked away.

I couldn't believe it. I was a dead man either way.

This can't be happening. I'm too young to die, I thought, as I walked the long hallway back to class. Even though my head was filled with thoughts of becoming gator bait, I actually felt sort of bad for the redhead. I mean, the guy didn't do anything. I did.

Maybe I should stop and think about the things I do before I do them? I'm not a baby anymore. But sometimes I get an idea in my head that really seems great. It really does! But I don't always think about how it will affect others. Maybe I should do that from now on?

Chapter 3

When I got home from school, I walked past my little sister Abby. She's in preschool. She's a goofball and a real pain. Abby asked me to say hi to her doll, Baby Cakes.

"I'm not saying hello to that stupid rag!" I yelled.

"She's not a rag!" Abby screamed before crying like a baby.

"Mommy, Michael called Baby Cakes a rag again," she shouted, as her eyes bugged out and her face turned red.

Mom stuck her head out of the kitchen and told me to watch it.

"Watch what?" I asked, looking around the room.

"Watch that mouth of yours before it gets you into more trouble, Michael."

"Whatever," I mumbled and walked to my room.

"And you'd better not slam that door," Mom said.

How did she know I was about to slam it shut?

Mom didn't know my mouth had already gotten me into trouble. Now there was no way out. I was doomed. I suppose I could have confessed right then, but I know Mom would have gotten so mad at me. I don't need that. I really, really wish I could go back in time and un-throw that rock. Surely there had to be a way out, right? What could I do? What could I do?

Aha! I had another great idea.

I decided to turn my room into a fortress with barricades and secret passages (how cool is that!) and all kinds of escape routes. It would be impossible to break into. Impossible, unless you were an angry alligator with ten million sharp, spikey teeth!

"If this doesn't work, I'm going to die. I don't

want to die! I don't want to die," I begged as I fell to my knees. Just then, my big brother Joey burst into my room, laughing his head off. He's 12 and likes to boss me and Abby around.

"What's so funny?" I asked.

"I don't want to die! I don't want to die!" he squealed as he dropped on his knees and pretended to cry. Joey had spied on me—again!

"Stop spying on me and get out," I warned him, "or I'll tell Dad you hit me."

"That's a lie! I didn't hit you," Joey shouted.

"So? Dad doesn't know that."

"What are you so scared of anyway, Mikey."

"I'm not afraid of anything."

"Well, it sounds like you're afraid of dying."

"Um, no," I stuttered. "I was just practicing for this play I'm in next week. "It's called, um, I forget what it's called."

Next week's play is *You Are What You Eat.* I play an onion—how stinky is that? Unfortunately, the onion doesn't have a big, dramatic death scene where it gets sliced and diced. If it had, that could have been my excuse.

Joey didn't believe me anyway.

"It's called *You're Not Telling The Truth And I Can Tell.* You're lying. I have a Michael's-lying-again-feeling in my gut," he said smugly and then strutted out of the room.

Joey's such a jerk, but he was right. I was lying. But so what? Either an angry redhead or an angry alligator was about to kill me.

I pretended to be asleep when Dad came to my room and said it was time for bed. He turned off the light and closed the door.

I waited a little before I got up and started to read my collection of *Encyclopedia Brown* books. (Now that I think about it, maybe I should have read *Pinocchio*.)

I planned to stay up all night. That way, I'd be able to spot the gator and call for help before he attacked.

I almost drifted off to sleep twice. Luckily, I was jolted awake;

once when the books fell to the floor and made a thud and later when my head hit the floor. Ouch!

Staying up until you see the sun again is really hard!

Between chapters, I got up and looked out my window to make sure the alligator wasn't creeping around the house. To get a better view, I tiptoed down the hall to the den. Boy was I glad to be on the second floor. Alligators are strong, and I'm sure this one could climb any wall.

For a split second, I freaked out when I saw something dart underneath the bushes. It turned out to be a raccoon. It startled me anyway, and I jumped back and tripped over my new Xbox. I fell and hit my head (again!) on the nightstand.

When I stood up, I was woozy. Even worse, I broke the Xbox! My poor Xbox was dead, and I was to blame. Ugh!

"Poor thing, you never did anything to deserve that," I whispered, petting it gently. I said goodbye to the Xbox and slowly crept back to bed where I spent the night worrying about where that gator might be.

Chapter 4

The sun finally rose, and I was still awake!
But when I heard Mom outside my door, I pretended I was asleep.

"Rise and shine!" she said, turning on the lights.

"Oh, not yet," I grumbled and faked a yawn. "I'm still sleeping."

That was another lie added to my growing list. I really don't like lying to my mom, but I had to. Well, I thought I had to.

"Okay, five more minutes and that's it," Mom said.

Wow, I should be an actor when I grow up. I gave a really terrific performance and fooled

Mom. I wonder if they give golden statues to kids who lie and throw things at helpless animals? Probably not.

When I got on the bus, I sat next to Kenny like always.

"Hey, what's up?" he said. Kenny's a guy who's always SOOOOO happy in the morning. I mean always! It's annoying!

"Not much. I'm just going to die is all. Been nice knowing you."

"Why are you talking crazy, Mikey?"

"I'm not talking crazy. I'm talking about how that big redheaded fifth-grader I blamed for throwing the rock is going to beat the crap out of me."

"Yikes. He's a big dude. I wouldn't want to be on the receiving end of his knuckle sandwich."

"Thaaaanks," I grumbled. "That makes me feel sooooo much better."

"You're welcome! Besides, he's probably forgotten all about you," chirped Kenny in his cheerfully annoying tone.

"I doubt it. And even if he did, the gator's gonna get me."

"What? How can an alligator get you in your house?"

"Duh, Kenny! Don't you know that alligators take their revenge at night when their victims are sleeping? Didn't you read the little sign in front of the alligator pond, the one with all the species facts on it?"

"No, Mikey, I didn't. I was too busy watching you throw a rock at that gator!"

"Shhhhh!" I whispered and quickly glanced around. "Everyone will hear you. You're supposed to lean in and whisper secret stuff like that, you know, like they do in the movies."

The bus ride lasted forever, and I was super tired. I fell asleep in the seat, and Kenny had to wake me when we got to school.

"Get up!" Kenny shouted, shaking me.

"Oh, wow. I'm so sleepy," I mumbled. "How am I going to make it through the day?"

"You'd better not nap in Miss Mitchell's class," Kenny warned me. "She can be scarier than all the fifth-graders and alligators combined!"

ZZZZZ

Chapter 5

When I got to my first class, I was so sleepy
I could barely walk straight.

We all had to sit in a circle and talk about our
zoo trip. Harriett, the biggest teacher's pet ever,
talked first and sat right next to me. Yuck!

"I love the koala because it's so cuddly and
cute and moves so slowly. I'm sure I'll get one
for Christmas," she bragged in her heavy English
accent. Spit flew out of her mouth and hit my arm.
YUCK! She's so gross and such a nerd!

The next thing I remember, Kenny was pinch-
ing me.

"What the heck did you do that for?" I angrily
whispered through clenched teeth.

"You're gonna get it if Miss Mitchell sees you napping," Kenny whispered back.

"Miss Mitchell, Kenny and Michael are talking and not listening to me," said smug and snobby Harriett. She had a wicked grin on her face. She loved getting us in trouble.

"Boys, remember our class rule about respecting others? Be sure to listen when others are speaking," Miss Mitchell reminded us. She gave us the old stink eye, too. You know, the one all teachers give you when they're NOT happy!

"Yes, Miss Mitchell," Kenny and I said at the same time.

Right before lunch was "read aloud." Miss Mitchell read a book about a crazy talking bird that did silly things. I was bored. I'd rather be eaten by the gator or beaten by the redhead than listen to any more of that story.

All of a sudden, I heard a voice say, "Michael! Michael McMichaels! Wake up! WAKE UP!"

Everyone was laughing.

I opened my eyes and looked around. Did I fart? Oops, I'm not supposed to say that word. Did I pass gas and not know it? Did I have a boog--, I mean, a bat in the cave?

"What's going on?" I yawned. "Are we done with that bird book yet?"

"What's going on is that you fell asleep on Harriett's shoulder. That's the second rule you've broken today," Miss Mitchell said in her stern teacher's voice. "No sleeping in class, Michael! Please walk directly to the principal's office."

"Michael likes Harriet! Michael likes Harriet!

Michael and Harriett sitting in a tree K-I-S-S-I-N-G," sang Martin Mooney as I got up to leave.

"Martin, silence! And that goes for all of you. Quiet down now, please," ordered Miss Mitchell.

I left the room and shuffled slowly down the hall. I could still hear my classmates.

"I think Michael is an alien, Miss Mitchell," Harriett said. "You'd better report him to NASA and the FBI. He likes me, and now I'm afraid he's going to take me back to his planet to conduct experiments on me. He lives on my block, you know. I need police protection. We can search his backyard for his spaceship. I'm sure it's there!"

Crud! What a mess I got myself into. Why did I throw that stupid rock? And why did I lie? If I had just told the truth and then apologized to Miss Mitchell, the redhead, and the alligator, I wouldn't be sleepy or scared.

My life stinks!

Chapter 6

In Principal Stein's office, I admitted to falling asleep during the read aloud.

"Really?" he said. "You know school is for learning and not for sleeping, Michael?"

"I guess. I mean, yes, I know that. It's just that I'm really tired and sometimes school's boring. I'm sorry, it just is," I said.

Principal Stein gave a quick smile then looked serious again and asked me why I was so tired.

"I was up late last night," I answered. "In fact I didn't sleep a wink."

"What were you doing?"

Good grief! I couldn't tell him I was afraid of being eaten by an angry gator because then he'd want to know why. I had to come up with something to say, something good, but something that wouldn't hurt anyone this time; a harmless little white lie.

I looked at Principal Stein and said, "Um, I was folding clothes and cleaning the bathroom all night. You know it's important to have clean clothes, right?"

I knew he wouldn't believe me if I told him what really happened. I mean, what third-grader stays up to read ALL NIGHT LONG?

Principal Stein then asked me if my mom had made me stay up to do those things for her.

In my most serious voice, I answered, "Yeah, you know she works. She can't do it all alone. She needs help. And Dad doesn't do a thing around the house. He's lazy, and his feet stink."

Principal Stein looked impressed. I thought he was going to tell me I'd win the "Helping Hand Award" at the next assembly. Instead, he told me he'd be back in a jiffy.

Alone in his office, I looked around but didn't see anything special. He had a couple of plants and some pictures of mountains and an ocean, or what looked like a big blob of water. There was a poster on the wall of a guy climbing a cliff. Below the climber's dangling body was the word, "P E R S E V E R A N C E." Must be a fancy word for crazy, I thought. Why would you climb a mountain when you can just look at a picture? I don't get it.

Behind his desk were photos of his family. His kids looked normal, but they had big teeth like the beavers we saw at the zoo.

When Principal Stein returned, the school counselor, Fannie Pharfuffle, was with him.

Miss Pharfuffle sat down next to me, which was weird. She asked me to describe my home life. That seemed weird too.

As a joke, I said, "My home doesn't have a life, Miss Pharfuffle." She smiled but didn't laugh. She looked me right in the eyes and slowly and softly said, "Michael, tell me about the chores your mother makes you do for her at night."

Her voice sounded different. I wondered if that's how everyone who goes to school counselor school talked.

I told her exactly what I told Principal Stein, only I couldn't remember which chores I'd said I'd done. That's the hard part about lying—remembering the lies. It's probably easier for your memory and your life to just tell the truth.

"Okay, Michael. Thank you very much. You can return to class now," Miss Pharfuffle said, looking kind of sad or serious or something. I was just glad to get out of there!

I walked back to class, minding my own business, when the nasty redheaded fifth-grader stepped out of the shadows. His jeans were ripped, and he had a chain around his neck that looked like a dog collar.

I froze.

"So, that gator hasn't gotten you yet. He's probably resting up so he can shred you apart tonight. Too bad for him, though, cause I'm going to do it now and there won't be anything left!" he said with his fist in the air.

I closed my eyes and waited for the punch. And waited. And waited. And waited. But nothing happened. Then a familiar voice echoed down the hall... it was Kenny! He was holding a hall pass and said Miss Mitchell was looking for me. I knew there was a reason why Kenny was my best friend!

"Well, I gotta get back to class. My teacher probably thinks I was kidnapped. I'm sure the police will be here any second. Wow! There they are now," I said and pointed toward the door.

When the redhead turned to look, I took off like a cheetah. I was almost to my classroom when a hand touched my shoulder. I screamed and dashed into the nearest room. It was Miss McCormick's fourth-grade class. She was a nice teacher, unless you screamed and disrupted her lesson.

"What on earth is going on?" Miss McCormick demanded to know as she put her hand on her chest. Had I given her a heart attack?

I really had to think fast. The whole class was staring at me.

"Um, I... I... saw a mouse... no, a rat... in the

hallway and I... I got scared. I mean it could have rabies, right?" I said.

Yep. I lied again! This had to be the third or fourth whopper I told that morning, but I'd lost count.

The big redhead stood in the hallway. He was snorting mad. His fists were raised like he wanted to box.

"Well, thank you for letting us know," Miss McCormick said before she called the main office and reported the "rat."

Principal Stein quickly showed up, and I told him what I "saw." I said it looked as big as a baby alligator, and that maybe it was an alligator that had escaped from the zoo.

"Well, I have a feeling it wasn't a gator, Michael," Principal Stein sighed. "I'll tell the janitor to set a few traps. Hopefully, that will be the end of it. Now get back to class."

Chapter 7

The school day was about to end when my name was called over the loud speaker. A voice told me to come to the office. Right then a couple classmates chanted, "Michael's in trouble! Michael's in trouble!"

Miss Mitchell ordered them to quiet down.

When I got to Principal Stein's office, I saw him, my mom, and the school counselor lady Fannie Pharfuffle.

Mom did NOT look happy. She told Principal Stein that ever since I came back from the zoo, I'd been acting strange.

"What's going on, Michael? Why did you tell everyone I made you do chores all night long?" Mom asked.

Before I could spit out one word, the counselor lady jumped in and said, "It's okay, Michael, you can tell us." She talked really slowly, like I was from another planet and didn't understand Earth language.

I took a deep breath and said, "Well, you see, I'm sort of scared of something."

"What? What are you afraid of sweetie?" Mom asked as she rubbed my hand.

That was my chance to finally tell the truth. But I didn't. I chickened out because I knew I'd get in big trouble. Mom and Dad would ground me for sure! They wouldn't let me go to Kenny's go-kart birthday party if they found out I was a big liar. And I LOVE racing go-karts as much as I love making secret tunnels. My heart raced, and my cheeks were red and hot like fire. My head must have looked like a fat tomato with a wig on top.

After a long silence, I nervously said, "Okay. The truth is I'm afraid of someone breaking into our house and kidnapping me. I saw a show about kidnapping the night before the zoo trip. It was really spooky and sad."

"Oh, honey," Mom said, hugging me. "That was just a show. You're safe here. Nobody is going to take you away." Then Mom kissed my cheek and hugged me even tighter.

I hate it when Mom gets all kissy-kissy and huggy-huggy. I'm not a baby!

Principal Stein and Fannie Pharfuffle agreed with Mom and told me I was being a worrywart... whatever that is.

How many lies had I told now? I really had lost count. What a mess!

Chapter 8

Friday night after dinner, Kenny came for a sleep over.

"Man, I can't believe your parents let me come over. Aren't you in trouble for falling asleep in class and getting sent to the principal's office?" Kenny asked.

"It's all good," I said.

Kenny was shocked.

"Really? So what happened in the principal's office?"

I was tired of thinking about it, but Kenny kept nagging me for details. That's when I started to think about what Kenny and I would be doing now if I hadn't thrown the rock and lied about it. We'd probably be laughing, playing video games, or talking about dinosaurs. Or maybe I'd be showing off my Japanese pencil cases. They're awesome! Each one has lots of secret compartments. Anyway, I'm sure we'd be doing something tons more fun than reliving the mess I made.

I told Kenny how sad and worried my mom looked when I said I was afraid of getting kidnapped in my sleep.

"You shouldn't lie to your Mom, Mikey. You should have just told the truth," Kenny said, as if he NEVER lies.

"We need to finish building this fort before it's too late," I replied, hoping to change the subject. "Let's not talk about that other stuff. It's over now."

Talking about what happened made my heart race. It did that every time I talked or thought about the bad things I'd done. The funny thing is, when I do the right things, like helping Mom make dinner or helping Joey clean his room, I never feel awful. Doing what's right makes me feel good. I wonder if that's true for everybody?

Kenny and I worked on the fort for hours.

I LOVE forts! We grabbed pillows, sheets, and chairs and built a fort with lots of hiding places. We even had a secret passage that led to a space behind my desk.

"Oh!" blurted Kenny, "I almost forgot to tell you something.

"What?" I asked.

"The redheaded fifth-grader who's going to beat you up is super tough. His name's Erik. My neighbor's cousin is in his class and told me stories about him. He beats people up all the time. It's like his job. One time he even…"

"Ugh!" I shouted. "Don't tell me. Let's just go watch TV, okay?"

Kenny's news made my heart nearly jump from my chest. I wanted to cry, but I wasn't going to look like a wimp in front of my best friend.

"Sure. But you messed up big time when you blamed him for throwing that rock. I mean, I think Erik's really going to beat you up," Kenny said.

"Well, the gator will probably get me first. I've got the whole weekend ahead of me, and I don't know if I'm going to make it."

"You know Mikey, I don't want to die either," Kenny admitted, looking a little scared. "What if that gator comes for you tonight but eats me instead? I don't wanna die, Mikey. I'm not ready! I haven't even been to Paris yet! My uncle says French people smoosh their lips together like fish when they talk. I want to see that! I gotta get out of here!"

I begged Kenny to stay and blocked the door.

"You can't leave! "You won't die, I promise. We built this fort so the alligator can't find us, duh!"

"Gators are really strong, Mikey. I don't want to die. And it'll hurt. Why didn't you just say you threw the rock?" Kenny whined.

"Because Miss Mitchell would have told my mother, and I would have been punished. Who wants to be punished?"

Chapter 9

Yes! I convinced Kenny to stay.

We took turns sleeping so one of us was always on watch and no one had to be up all night. That was my idea. I got it from a movie I saw at my grandfather's house. I love watching movies with Gramps.

I volunteered to sleep first. Kenny didn't mind taking first watch, but he threatened to sue me if he woke up dead. His dad was a lawyer, and Kenny loved to use law lingo.

"You can't SUE me; my name's Michael, not Sue," I joked.

"Yeah! Real funny, Mikey," Kenny shot back as he lifted the binoculars to his eyes.

The next thing I remember, Kenny was shaking me and shouting. I tried to ignore him, but he kept shaking me and shining a flashlight in my face.

I thought I heard Kenny say, "Wake up, Mikey, I have to get to sleep." But then I heard a roar and felt a bite on my arm.

"The gator got in, Mikey! It's over!" shouted Kenny.

I screamed and did karate chops with my arms and legs, just like the ones I saw in that movie about a teen and his Japanese teacher. (The two liked to catch flies with chopsticks. Weird!) I kara-te-chopped and kicked like crazy.

"Look out, alligator, here comes Michael McMichaels. HHHIIIYYYAAA!" I screamed.

That's when I saw Kenny curled up on the floor, crying. A second later, the bedroom door flung open, the lights came on, and my parents, in their pajamas, hurried inside.

"What's going on in here?" Dad barked. "Why are you two fighting?"

"Kenny, are you okay?" Mom asked, as she knelt down and touched his shoulder.

"Oh noooo! I'm dead. I'm dead, and I'm suing ALL of you!" Kenny whimpered.

Mom and Dad started laughing, and Kenny looked confused.

"What's so funny about me being dead?"

"Nothing at all, Kenny," Mom answered as she doubled over with laughter. "Are you Okay?"

"Yeah, I guess so."

Kenny sat on my bed and held his stomach.

"You boys get to bed, or this will be the last sleep over ever," Dad warned us before slamming the door shut.

"Mikey, why did you go crazy on me?"

"I thought you were the gator, Kenny! Why did you bite me?"

"Because you wouldn't wake up!"

The situation was so wild and weird, we both laughed until we fell asleep in the fort.

Chapter 10

The next morning, Dad cooked a big breakfast for the whole family plus Kenny. We ate French toast, pancakes, scrambled eggs, bacon, sausage, and orange juice. (The adults drank coffee.)

In my best English accent, I said, "I would like some coffee, please."

"It'll stunt your growth," Dad answered and then put a giant pile of pancakes on the table.

"No, it won't. You always say that. Besides, I'm already almost an adult," I said, before smearing butter on my cakes.

"You're funny, NOT!" Joey said. "Just because you have a girlfriend doesn't mean you're an adult. And don't hog all the butter."

"Shut up. I don't have a girlfriend!"

"Hee-hee! Mikey has a girlfriend! Mikey has a girlfriend!" Abby said in a sing-song voice. Then she made a loud kissing sound and stuck out her tongue.

"Shut up, Abby! I do not!"

"Settle down Michael. Don't tell your sister or brother to shut up," Dad told me in his stern Dad voice. "And someone pass the syrup, please."

"What's this about a girlfriend, Mikey?" Mom asked from the kitchen.

"Her name's Harriet, soon-to-be Harriett McMichaels," Joey answered, laughing. "It's all over school!"

I was so mad, I almost lost it. Everyone thought Harriett and I were a couple just because my head was on her shoulder after I accidentally fell asleep during read aloud. How stupid and gross!

Joey kept laughing and pointing at me from across the table, so I threw a pancake at his face. It smacked him good. Butter and syrup ran down his cheek.

Joey leapt out of his chair screaming,

"You're dead, lover boy!"

Lucky for me, Dad stopped him. Joey was so mad, I think he would have punched me in the eye. Dad made him sit down and apologize. What a mess!

Chapter 11

After breakfast, Dad drove Kenny and me to our baseball game—the biggest one of the season.

We were ahead 4 to 3 in the bottom of the ninth inning against the best team in the league. Victory was at hand!

I was in left field waiting for the next batter when I suddenly got a sick feeling in the pit of my stomach. Had I eaten too many pancakes? Nope! I had just caught a glimpse of the big bad redhead, a.k.a. Erik. He was leaning against the left field fence, and he seemed to be talking to me. But I couldn't hear a word he said.

I stared in his direction, trying to read his lips. Finally, I understood. He was mouthing, "You're gonna get it!"

I pointed at myself and said, "Me?" Erik nodded his head up and down real slow, and then he raised his fist.

I was so busy keeping my eyes on him, I forgot about the game... until I heard all the screaming.

I don't know what happened, but Miguel Diaz, our center fielder, was beside me. He picked up the baseball by my foot and heaved it to home plate. The throw was late. Two runs scored, and it was game over. We lost 5 to 4. The winners celebrated in a huge dog pile at home plate.

I walked back to the dugout totally confused. My teammates stared at me. The really angry ones glared.

"What happened out there, Mikey?" coach asked. "Why didn't you go for the ball?"

I didn't answer. I sat by myself in the dugout. A few minutes passed before Braden Brighton, our team captain, stopped and talked to me.

"Look, I know you have a girlfriend now, but you have to keep your head in the game," Braden told me.

I looked straight at him and said, "I don't have a girlfriend!"

"What about Harriett?" Braden asked. "That's what everybody's saying."

I tried really hard not to cry. But I did. I cried like a big baby. Someone should have given me a diaper.

Everything was screwed up! Will this gator mess ever end?

Chapter 12

When I got home from the game, I ran straight to my room. I passed Mom on the stairs but didn't say a word.

Outside my door, I heard her and Dad whispering.

"What's the matter with him?" Mom wanted to know.

"He had a bad day in the outfield. It was like he was somewhere else. I don't know what's gotten into him," Dad told her.

"I think I know," Mom said softly. "He's afraid someone will break into the house and take him. He saw it happen on a TV show, and it's scared him to death."

There was a long pause and then Dad said, "Gee, if he's that scared, maybe we should go ahead and get that alarm system. It's expensive, but it might be just the thing to help him feel safe."

Later that night, I decided to write my will. A will is important, at least that's what the old dude in the TV commercial screams. He'll write one for you, and do it cheap! But since I don't have any money, I had to do it myself.

I have a lot of stuff. If I don't say who gets what, Kenny, Joey, and Abby will fight over everything!

THE WILL OF
MICHAEL MCMICHAELS,
3RD-GRADER:

I leave all of my video games and books to my best friend Kenny. My brother, Joey, can have my Super Soaker and my collection of action figures. Even though we fight a lot, I still kind of love him. My sister, Abby, gets the gold crucifix I got for First Communion last year. (If Grandpa wants it back, then Abby can have my pencil case. It's from Japan and cost like $25. We had to drive to New York City to get it.) My parents can have my baby pictures. I know they're not worth a lot of money, but Mom and Dad have jobs so money shouldn't matter.

Everything else that I didn't mention goes to any charity that helps boys killed by alligators or by scary fifth-graders named Erik. They died because they threw rocks at alligators, lied, and blamed others. There has to be a charity like that in this big country of ours.

I signed my name and then put the will on top of my desk where I knew it would be found. Then I searched for my football uniform. I figured I should wear pads and a helmet to bed in case the gator paid a visit.

I found the uniform stuffed in the back of the closet. I stretched as far as I could just to touch it. That's when I had another awesome idea! I'd wear my uniform AND sleep in the closet!

If the gator did come, I'd fool him. I stuffed a bunch of towels under the bedsheets so it looked like I was under the covers. Then I put my baseball cap on the pillow. Munch on that angry alligator!

Before I crawled into the closet, I opened the bedroom window as wide as I could. I had to make sure the gator got in and chewed those towels. Then it would all be over, or sort of. I still had Erik the redhead after me, but I had to solve one problem at a time.

I crawled to the back of the closet. It was cozy. Lots of old blankets and pillows were piled on the floor, plus all the clothes that had fallen off their hangers. No way could the gator or anyone else see me. I quickly drifted off to sleep.

In the morning, I was jolted awake by scream-ing. My mom was shouting her baby boy had been stolen... kidnapped! She was in a complete panic. I heard Dad trying to comfort her and calm her down.

I should have crawled out of the closet right then. But I didn't. I was scared. I knew I'd be in BIG trouble.

The shrill sound of sirens filled the air. Someone had called the police!

I heard footsteps everywhere. Strange voices asked my parents all kinds of questions. Then I heard barking. Barking? Something was clawing at the closet door.

I curled into a ball and freaked out. Suddenly, the door opened and light flooded the closet. A bright light hit my face. I was blinded. Something licked my nose.

"Are you okay, little guy?" a strange, husky voice asked me.

"I'm okay. Tell everyone I'm fine," I said.

When I crawled out, it was like a scene from a

movie. My parents, brother, and sister rushed me. They hugged me so tight, I could barely breathe. Everyone was crying...even my brother!

"Little bro, forget about hitting me with that soggy pancake. I forgive you," Joey blurted out as he wiped away tears.

Then Dad said, "Michael, we thought you'd been kidnapped!"

Before I could say anything, Mom asked me if I was hiding in the closet because I was scared someone would break into the house. I nodded yes. All I wanted to do was tell the truth, but I didn't. I was afraid of being punished and having my siblings and the police know I was a liar and a fake.

Kenny was right. I should have admitted to throwing the rock when Miss Mitchell asked me. Even better, I should never have thrown the stupid rock in the first place.

Mom hugged me again and said not to worry. Mom and Dad were going to put in an alarm. They were going to spend hundreds of dollars just for me. Wow! They really loved me, and I still lied to them.

I felt sick again. My cheeks were on fire. Life was so much easier and carefree before all this gator mess. How much more stinky could my life get!

Chapter 13

Hours after the police, and their pooch, had cleared out and all was calm again, Kenny called. I was doing homework and feeling awful.

"Is it true? Seriously, I heard the police swarmed your house today! Did they have their guns drawn? Did anyone get shot?" Kenny asked so many questions, I couldn't think.

How did he find out so fast?

"It's all over the neighborhood, Mikey," continued Kenny. "Just like the news about you and Harriett."

"Who cares! We're getting an alarm today, so I won't have to worry about that stupid alligator anymore."

"What about Erik? He wants to fight you at school? Aren't you afraid of him?" Kenny wondered.

"Gee, Kenny, I sort of forgot about that. Thanks for the reminder," I snapped.

"Sure! See you on the bus tomorrow!"

After I hung up on Kenny, Mom walked into my room and told me to wear my good pants. It was Grandma's birthday, and we were headed to her house for dinner.

The drive to Grandma's was uneventful until we turned onto her street. Erik and his buddies were riding their bikes, and they rode right next to our car. Man, they're fast!

When we pulled into Grandma's driveway, Erik and his crew stopped in the middle of the street. I got out of the car and quickly looked back at them. Erik shouted, "You're dead!" He said it over and over again.

I froze right there in the driveway with Grandma's birthday present in my hands.

"Michael be careful with that," Mom warned me as she walked to Grandma's front door. I stepped forward really slowly. I moved so slow, everyone else had gone in the house and I was still on the driveway. I crept along until I saw a rock whiz past my head. I dropped Grandma's gift and ran to the door.

Erik and his friends laughed and pedaled away. Mom met me at the door and saw the gift shattered on the driveway.

I whimpered, "I'm sorry, Mom. Really I am. I'm such an idiot."

"It's okay, Michael. I know you're nervous and accidents happen," she said, rubbing my head.

Then Grandma stepped forward with words of encouragement.

"Don't be upset, Michael," she said. "I know you've had a lot to deal with."

How did Grandma know? My heart pounded, and my cheeks turned red—again!

"Your momma told me all about it. Don't you worry, champ, it's all going to be okay. No kidnapper is going to take my grandson."

Ugh! Now I even had poor Grandma fooled. Will anything I do make this all go away?

Chapter 14

After the birthday disaster at Grandma's, I went to bed. I tossed and turned for hours. Finally, I decided to say a prayer. I never prayed unless I was at church, but this was serious.

"I hope you're listening. I know you don't hear from me very much, but I'm in a mess. I know I've been bad, but I really didn't mean for any of it to happen. I hate seeing my family all freaked out. I also hate that everyone at school thinks I like Harriett. Can you tell the alligator to go to Harriett's house instead? Just kidding! I need a miracle! I need a miracle!" I repeated over and over.

After finally falling asleep, I had the worst nightmare of my life!

I dreamt the gator crawled through my window and chased me out the front door and around the block. I was running in my purple polka dot underwear and screaming my head off. Just as I was about to become snack food, a deep voice pierced the darkness, "You're dead, kid!"

Nooooooooo. Erik and fifty of his crazy friends were pedaling toward me, laughing, and pointing at my underwear. Erik yelled, "Who wears purple baby underwear? Does baby need his diaper changed?" I kept running and running and running. Then I woke up. It was 3:30 in the morning.

Scared and covered in sweat, I crawled under the bed with my Super Soaker for protection.

"Time to get up, Michael!" It's time for school. Get out from under the bed, now! Let's move it!" Mom shouted.

Half asleep, I opened my eyes but couldn't see a thing. It was total darkness.

"Um, Mom. I think I'm blind."

"What are you talking about, Mikey?"

"My eyes are open, and all I see is black. I'm BLIND! Oh no! Now I have to go to a special school and wear dark sunglasses and walk around with a big walking stick! Nooooooooo! I'll never see you again!"

Mom just laughed.

"Hey, it's not funny! Why are you laughing?" I demanded to know from under the bed.

"I have an idea that just might cure your blindness. It's experimental, but it just may work. Grab my hand."

I grabbed Mom's hand, and she yanked, tugged, and pulled. Soon enough, I could see! It was a miracle! (Or maybe the bright lights in the room helped a bit. Either way, I could see!)

Chapter 15

I climbed the stairs of the bus, and Kenny immediately said he had BIG news.

"Okay, let me have it," I said and braced for the worst.

"My neighbor's cousin Billy, you know, the one who knows Erik. He said Erik is going to mess you up today! Maybe you should just say you're sorry and confess everything. Or skip school."

"Are you nuts?" I yelled. "Then I'll get into all kinds of trouble for skipping. No way!"

It was rehearsal day for the big play; the one where I play an onion and Kenny is a carrot. We had to practice our dance moves for the final number.

The onion costume was a total pain. I looked

like the fattest, roundest kid on the planet. Plus it was a thousand degrees inside the thing!

"Okay, class. We're going to practice until we get it right. You don't want to disappoint all your family and friends, do you?" Miss Mitchell said with a big grin.

Maybe it was time for her to retire if she thought singing and dancing vegetables were entertaining. I stood on stage with the whole cast, all of us looking like total dorks, when Erik strutted into the auditorium.

He stared at me as he walked toward Miss Mitchell and told her Principal Stein had to see me.

"Okay, Michael. Principal Stein wants to see you in his office. Go with Erik," she ordered.

Harriett, who was dressed like a cucumber, smirked and said, "Ha-ha! You're gonna get it now!" Then she stuck out her fat ugly tongue.

"Shut up, freak!" I said. "I hope someone chops you up and sticks you in a salad!"

I looked at Kenny in his bright orange carrot costume as I walked off the stage. He waved and whispered, "Bye Mikey. Nice knowing you."

Erik followed me out of the auditorium.

Lucky for me, Miss Wong's second-grade class was in the hallway. I walked next to them and just smiled at Erik. He couldn't do a thing to me as long as they were there.

"Uh, excuse me, Mr. Onion. Where are you going?" Miss Wong asked.

"I'm going to Principal Stein's office," I answered.

"Well you'll never get there if you follow us. We're going in the opposite direction. Surely you know where the principal's office is by now," Miss Wong said.

I looked at Erik. He had a big "I-got-you" grin on his face. It was time to run.

I must have been the fastest onion ever! I ran up the hallway and down the stairs, screaming past every classroom.

"Help! Help! Somebody call 911! Call the president! Send the army and the navy! HHHEEELLLPPP,"

I screamed before I tripped over a pink backpack. (I'm sure it belonged to yucky Harriett – Ugh!)

I didn't fall flat on my face. Instead, I bounced and rolled. I was like an onion bowling ball. I rolled all the way down the hall and through the doors of the main office. I didn't stop until I smacked into the secretary's desk. I was so dizzy, I was ready to barf!

Principal Stein was standing over me, but I couldn't get up because of the stupid costume. All I could do was wiggle side to side.

"I'd like to see you in my office, Michael" he said.

"But I can't get up, Mr. Stein. I really can't!"

Principal Stein took a deep breath, grabbed my hands, and pulled me up. Then off to his office we went.

"Michael, tell me what's really going on. How did you end up rolling into the office like that?"

I panicked and blurted out the first thing that popped into my head.

"Well, I was walking to the bathroom when a big gust of wind knocked me over. I mean, I think it was a hurricane!"

Principal Stein didn't buy it.

"Is that what really happened, or are you making up a story, Michael?"

"Um, Mr. Stein. I think I'm going to throw up."

And then it happened. I spewed all over his office. Yuck! My heart raced, my face felt like it was on fire, and my voice trembled. I FINALLY knew it had to end!

"I'm a liar. I lied about everything! I'll tell you the truth now, I promise! I'm sick of lying," I sobbed.

Chapter 16

I told Principal Stein the whole, horrible story. Every fib. Every untruth. Every exaggeration. Every mistake.

He listened and never said a word. Then he called Erik to his office and asked him why he had threatened me.

"Well, Mr. Stein, Michael started it. He lied and said I hit the gator with the rock. My teacher called my mom, and I got punished!" Erik was sniffling, and a tear drop raced down his cheek.

"What Michael did was very wrong, but does that mean you can follow him around, put your fists in his face, and tell him he's going to die?"

"Well, yeah. I mean no. I mean... I don't know, Mr. Stein?" Erik mumbled.

"I'm calling both of your parents. But before I do, we need to have a chat about truth telling and proper comportment."

"What's proper comportment?" I asked Principal Stein.

"Comportment is your conduct or how you act, Michael. You do realize it was wrong to throw a rock at the gator, don't you? Even if it didn't hurt him, that's unacceptable."

Principal Stein stood up from his desk, rolled up his sleeves, and towered over us.

"Do you understand what I'm saying, Michael? You made things worse by lying to Miss Mitchell and everyone else about what you did. Erik behaved quite well at the zoo and didn't deserve to be falsely accused."

I looked at Erik, and he had a wide grin on his face. He loved watching me squirm.

"And that brings me to you, Erik," Principal Stein continued. "You're not exactly innocent either."

Now Erik squirmed.

"Telling Michael you'd beat him up was an

awful thing to say. You also lied when you said the gator would eat him in his sleep. I'm sure you wanted to scare him, but you can't go around scaring and bullying other students. Do you understand, Erik? Michael, do you understand? Are we all on the same page now?"

"Yes, Mr. Stein. Throwing the rock and lying about it was wrong. I'm sorry, and I won't do it again," I said.

And I meant it, too. A tear even rolled down

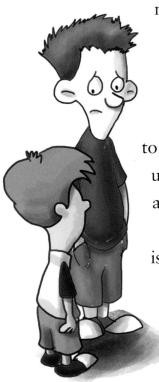

my cheek. But my cheeks weren't burning, and my heart wasn't pounding. I had finally found peace and calm!

Principal Stein turned back to Erik and asked him again if he understood that threatening me and scaring me was wrong.

"Yes, Mr. Stein, I do. I promise not to do it again."

I looked straight at Erik to try and figure out if he really meant it. I think he did. He was upset, just like me. He looked like a guy who felt so bad, he wouldn't dare do it again.

Principal Stein wasn't done. He called Kenny to the office and questioned him about his behavior. He praised Kenny for listening to my problems and being a true friend. But he also had a warning. He told Kenny he should have told an adult, someone he trusted, about what was going on.

Kenny tried to defend his actions by telling Principal Stein he didn't want to be a tattletale. That's when our principal taught us the In/Out Rule. He said it's not okay to tell on someone for no reason, or if you just want to get someone "in" trouble. But if you're trying to keep someone safe or "out" of trouble, you should tell. He told us to follow that rule in the future. It made sense. He should probably teach Harriett the In/Out Rule. I doubt she'd follow it though. No one can tell her anything.

Kenny apologized and promised to do better in the future. We all did.

Chapter 17

When my mom and dad and Erik's mom and dad showed up to Principal Stein's office, I had to explain the whole thing over again. Ugh! When I was done, they all looked more disappointed than mad.

Erik and I had to apologize to each other– again. And we had to promise not to lie, bully, or threaten others in the future.

But it wasn't all bad. I found out gators can't escape from the zoo and break into your house. Gee, if I'd only known that last week!

Anyway, I was glad it was over. Well, mostly over. I was sure a big, nasty punishment was waiting for me at home.

Chapter 18

I was right. I got punished.

I wasn't allowed to play in any baseball games for two weeks... but I still had to go to all the practices. No TV, computer time, or video games either! Worst of all, I had to miss Kenny's go-kart birthday party.

And those were just the things I couldn't do! My parents also had me DO stuff!

I had to write apology letters to Erik, Principal Stein, Miss Mitchell, and the zookeeper. I even had to write an apology poem to the alligator! Gators can't read, can they? Oh well, it doesn't matter. I decided to be a zoo volunteer so I could read my poem to the gator.

Here's my apology poem to Rocky. Yep, I named the gator Rocky. I hope he likes his name as much as the poem!

I'm Sorry Rocky,

My name is Mikey, and
    I don't want to pout,
But I threw the rock
    that hit you in your snout.

I made a poor decision that
    left me sad, sick, and blue,
But getting hit by a stone
    was surely worse for you.

Little kids like me should behave
    at home and at the zoo,
Not tell lies or make big messes
    like I always do.

I'm so very sorry and promise it
    will never happen again.
I'll do whatever I have to,
    until I make amends!

*You were the victim of a
cowardly assault.
Please accept this apology,
for it truly was all my fault.*

That was my adventure... or misadventure! I am going to try really hard to tell the truth from now on. I know I won't be perfect, but I will always try my best!

Boys Town Press
Featured Titles

*Kid-friendly books
to teach social skills*

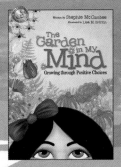

BOYS TOWN® Press

BoysTownPress.org

**For information on Boys Town,
its Education Model®,
Common Sense Parenting®,
and training programs:**
boystowntraining.org
boystown.org/parenting
EMAIL: training@BoysTown.org
PHONE: 1-800-545-5771

**For parenting and educational
books and other resources:**
BoysTownPress.org
EMAIL: btpress@BoysTown.org
PHONE: 1-800-282-6657